*To Matty
Happy reading
Simon Taylor*

Simon Taylor

Imogen and the Children from Undurbedd

Illustrated by Bemmigail

Text Copyright © Simon Taylor 2018

Illustrations Copyright © Simon Taylor 2018

The moral rights of the author have been asserted.

First edition October 2018. Published by Simon Taylor. Edited by Pitchfork Communications Ltd.

This is a work of fiction. Names, characters, places and incidents either are the product of the authors' imagination, or are used fictitiously, and any resemblance to actual persons, living or dead, business, companies, events or locales is entirely coincidental.

All rights reserved.

Without limiting the rights under copyright above, no part of this publication may be reproduced, stored in or introduced into a retrieval system, or transmitted, in any form or by means (electronic, mechanical, photocopying, recording or otherwise), without the prior written permission of both the copyright owner and the above publisher of this book.

www.simontaylorstoryteller.com

To Imogen

my Granddaughter.

For when she is older.

Chapter 1: The Visitors

Imogen lay in bed. She was exhausted. She had no brothers or sisters, but she didn't mind too much because her close friend Sue lived next door. They had been playing all evening in the fields behind their houses with Sue's dog Scratch. Imogen smiled, but she was so tired she couldn't concentrate on her memories. She yawned and drifted gently off to sleep.

Suddenly, she was awake again. The night was clear and the moonlight showed nothing was moving in her room. It was all quiet in the house; Mum and Dad must have switched the television off and gone to bed.

Then she heard it again. Except this time, she was wide awake. There was no mistake. She could hear whispering. She couldn't quite make out what was being said, but somehow it wasn't frightening, just odd. It sounded like two children's voices. They were arguing in loud whispers. Imogen sat up. The voices were coming from under her bed!

She carefully looked over the side bed and in the dim light she could see two little creatures or children even, creeping out from under the bed. They were not scary at all. They were tiptoeing, looking around the whole time. But they weren't children, because they were covered in fine, light-brown hair, had big eyes, a flat nose and large ears that seemed to twitch at the slightest noise. They had tiny horns on top of their heads.

Their shape was human but slightly broader and they both looked strong. Their eyes, full of colour, made them look friendly and kind. They were wearing dark coloured clothes and their bare legs had the same light-brown fur down to their bare feet. One had a voice higher than the other. Perhaps that was a girl, Imogen thought.

She wasn't afraid, because they were tiny. Not even as high as Imogen's knee, and she was only 10 years old. She watched, open mouthed in amazement, as the little girl put her hands on her hips and whispered, "You are going to get us into so much trouble. Norti by name and naughty by nature.

What happens if Wilmena the Wise catches us away from Underbedd?"

The little boy turned around and held his finger to his lips. "We are just going to scare the Ovurbedd girl who lives here and then go straight back. Honest, it'll be fun."

"Well," said the girl, looking around, "scaring people doesn't sound like fun to me."

Imogen moved slightly so she could see them better. At that moment they both turned around and looked straight up the bed. All they could see was a shape on the top of the bed. It appeared to have two round things in the middle, which suddenly blinked, then the whole shape moved! It was a face, a girl. A large girl to them. A giant, in fact.

They started to back away because it was the most important law; they must never be seen by the big people of Ovurbedd. It could be dangerous.

They both opened their mouths to scream, but nothing came out. The boy grabbed the girl and hugged her to him and they both stood still, trembling. Imogen lifted her head up so all her face was clear. She grinned and whispered, "Who are you?"

The little boy trembled and hid behind the little girl. Imogen thought it looked so funny, especially when she remembered he was there to try and frighten her. She started to giggle, she just couldn't help it!

The girl started to smile and, shaking off the little boy, put her hands to her mouth and started to giggle too. The boy stood back and just looked and felt a bit silly.

"Who are you?" Imogen asked again.

"My name is Corshus," said the girl, "and this is Norti." Imogen thought they were strange names but didn't mention it, in case it hurt their feelings.

"My name is Imogen. Why are you so little and why were you under my bed and," putting her head to one side and looking thoughtful, "I don't know you, so why were you trying to scare me?"

Norti looked shame-faced as Corshus turned around, looked at him and then crossed her arms, clearly waiting for him to explain.

He shifted his weight from one foot to the other and shrugged his shoulders.

"Dunno. And I'm not little, I'm as tall as any boy my age."

"Go on," said Corshus, "tell her it's a game you boys play and think is funny. Go on."

Norti looked a bit sheepish and then said to the floor.

"Well, you see all the boys do it once, you know, to show they are nearly men."

He looked up at Imogen.

"You have to pick a door and go and frighten a child of Ovurbedd. We pretend to be the monsters that are supposed to live under the bed. They don't really exist you see. We just do it for fun."

Imogen shifted around on the bed so she was more comfortable. She remembered her Mum and Dad could be upstairs and began to whisper.

"No monsters under the bed? Never?"

"Honest." Norti and Corshus both nodded together.

Imogen changed the subject.

"So, where's Ovurbedd?"

"Here," they both said together, opening their arms wide.

Corshus continued, "we live in Undurbedd," pointing beneath the bed. "We came through the Door of Shade to your world, Ovurbedd."

The boy shifted again on his feet.

"You're not going to punish us, are you? We're really sorry!"

The little girl turned to look at the boy and frowned, but said nothing. Imogen just laughed. "No, of course not."

Then she had a thought, leaned forward off the bed and in an excited whisper said, "so where is the door to Undurbedd?"

"If you come down here," said Corshus, "and look under your bed, you can see it."

Imogen scrambled off the bed, looked under it, and gasped. There, in the wall, nearly as tall as the base of Imogen's bed, was a door. It was slightly open and sunlight was peeking all around its edges. She was astonished because it wasn't there earlier when she put her slippers under the bed, and it *definitely* wasn't there yesterday when she was looking for a book.

Corshus saw her expression and began to explain. "It only appears if we come through it. Norti, we must go back before we get into trouble, goodbye Imogen!"

Before Imogen could say another word, Corshus grabbed Norti's hand and the two of them ran to the door. They waved goodbye and quickly rushed through the door and shut it tight. As soon as it shut, it disappeared. Now, the only light in the room was the moonlight.

Imogen kept looking at where the door had been, then slid under the bed and touched where she thought the door had been. There was no door, no door frame, just wall. Puzzled, she climbed into bed and lay there thinking and remembering. Because as Corshus and Norti went through the door, it was wide open. The sun had flooded in and behind them she could see the greenest of fields and trees. There was so much to think about; why were they so tiny? She wanted to stay awake, but the sheets felt warm and comfortable and they folded around her and...

* * *

"Imogen, time to get up!" It was her Dad. She woke up and squinted her eyes at the sun shining through her curtains. She lay there for a second and wondered whether it was all a dream. She jumped up and looked under the bed. No Undurbedders, no door. Just wall. She sighed and stood up thinking it must have been a dream, just a very, very real dream.

But then something sparkled in the sunlight by her toes. She bent down. There was a stone, the size of the stone in her mum's ring and she realised there was a gold chain holding it with a clasp at the ends. It was a necklace. As she bent down and picked it up, she realised the chain was broken. The little girl must have dropped it. But that meant the two children were real and last night did happen and it wasn't a dream.

Imogen was so excited, but knew she couldn't tell her Mum and Dad or even her friend Susie. She would keep it secret until she saw her best friend Roari. She put the necklace in her special box. It was covered in felt and glass-coloured stones. There she kept her most valuable things, like the bracelet Mum and Dad had bought her last Christmas. She wondered if the children would come back.

She didn't go out that day, but kept on thinking of reasons to rush upstairs and check under the bed, just in case. But there was no sign of them or the door. That night in bed, she was so excited that they may come back that it took ages for her to get comfortable and less fidgety. But they didn't come back. Nor the next day or night. As she drifted off to sleep on the third night, she had decided that they would not be coming back and that made her a little sad.

She was awake. Wide awake. It was dark. Something had woken her. Voices. There it was again! Whispered voices! It was the boy speaking.

"Well, where were you standing? Because if it's not here, perhaps the girl picked it up."

Corshus hissed back. "You must have knocked it off when you grabbed me. I was about here I think. Oh, I don't remember. I knew we shouldn't have come."

As she stood there and started to cry, Imogen looked over the edge of the bed.

"Hello, please don't cry. I found your necklace and have been keeping it safe for you."

The little girl went from sad to shock to a big smile of relief. Imogen jumped out of bed, took the delicate little necklace out of the box and sitting down on the floor beside them, gave it to the little girl. She took it and held it to her chest, a look of such relief on her face. Then she took Imogen's hand in hers and gave her smile of warmth and happiness and relief.

"Thank you, Imogen. This necklace is my Mum's. I really thought I had lost it."

Imogen smiled back at her. But she was also thinking how lovely the fur on her arms and hands was. It was so soft and warm.

"Come on Corshus," said Norti, "we should get going, if we are away much longer, we may not be so lucky this time."

Then he stopped and grinned up at Imogen. "But we are grateful, honest."

Imogen looked a little sad that they were going so soon. She had so many questions and wanted to know so much. Then she brightened up.

"Can I look through the door before you close it?"

The two children looked at each other and nodded to each other.

"Okay, but please be quick," said Norti.

They held each other's hands and ran under the bed towards the open door. Imogen grabbed her dressing gown because she was getting cold and slid under the bed. She gasped as Norti opened the door wide. She felt the sun on her face and warm air flow all around her. As her eyes adjusted to the brightness, she saw a notice on the door. It said: 'Imogen, aged 10. Long hair, brown eyes.' There was more but it was too small to read.

Corshus saw her reading. "Every child has a door from us to you in Ovurbedd and every door has a note about who you are. Wilmena the Wise says it has always been this way, because of the prophecy."

"What prophecy?" asked Imogen.

They looked at each other, then looked a bit embarrassed. Corshus spoke first.

"We don't know really - we just know that they have to be there."

Imogen didn't answer because she was looking behind and beyond Corshus. She just stared in amazement. Through the open door were green fields, trees and giant bushes, stretched out as far as the eye could see. It looked like the fields near her house, but everything was slightly different. The grass was greener, the trees taller. The bushes stood as tall as trees and some of them had big white flowers shaped like teardrops hanging down from the branches. The air smelt so sweet with the scent of the flowers and she could hear the chirping of so many different bird songs, but not like the bird songs she was used to in her garden. Just different. Imogen felt very excited and wished she was small enough to fit through the door.

Then, in the distance she saw a grown up coming towards them. Like Norti, but bigger. The stranger hadn't seen them but was looking around and behind him. He was wearing a brown shirt and leggings and riding a four-legged animal. It was red with a white flash on its chest and muzzle. As it came nearer, she realised it was a wolf, no, a fox. A huge fox!

Norti spotted it and gasped. "Quickly, before Creagh sees us." He smiled at Imogen, half waved and rushed through the open door. Corshus leant forward and kissed Imogen on the cheek. It felt warm and furry and funny and nice all at the same time.

"Take care and I promise, we will come back to visit you."

Before Imogen could speak she had gone through the door. It had shut, the light had gone, the door had gone, only her bedroom wall remained visible in the dim moon light. Slowly, she pushed herself out from under the bed and took off her dressing gown, all the time thinking about the strange and wonderful world she had just seen that lay behind the wall.

She climbed back into bed, suddenly exhausted. She had so much to think about. There was another world the other side of her bedroom wall and it was so different. She was excited but too tired to think. As she drifted off to sleep, her only thought was that she must tell Roari all about it.

Chapter 2 - Imogen tells Roari

The next day, Sunday, was sunny. Mum was in the garden and Dad had had to go to work even though it was a Sunday. That meant their day out had been cancelled. The sky was blue and it would have been fun, but Imogen wasn't sad. She had to tell someone about meeting the children from Undurbedd and she knew she couldn't tell her friends or Mum and Dad.

But Imogen was used to adventures. The Undurbedd children were not the first time she had come across magical things. She sat in her special place, behind the shed at the bottom of their long garden. It was next to fields and she loved the fact no one could see her. It was her place and she liked to sit in the sunshine and read there.

She held a stone in her hand. It was like half an egg that had been split down the middle, so one side was completely flat. It was black and completely smooth. It was a 'calling stone'. She had found it two years ago. She rubbed it and thought about her particular friend Roari, who had the other half. She whispered his name. "Roari - can you come, I've got something so exciting to tell you."

At first nothing happened, then the air and everything around her grew very still. Suddenly there was a rush of warm air, a flash and in front of her was a dragon. He was over 4 metres tall. Green scales covered his back, sides and long tail. They shone and flashed in the sunlight and his long, crimson wings seemed to hold the light as he folded them against his sides. Smoke curled out of his mouth and around his long nose when he spoke and although he looked fearsome, his large brown eyes were full of kindness.

"Hello Imogen," he said. He was chewing a large fish and the tail was sticking out of his mouth. His eyes smiled though and Imogen laughed.

"I'm sorry Roari, I didn't know you were having tea."

In his front claws were several other fish and he looked at them longingly, before sitting down on the grass next to the shed.

"It sounded important, so Mum said I could come straight away. What's happened?"

Imogen smiled up him. They had met when Imogen was 8 and he was just a young boy dragon. Time in his world worked differently and he was now a 'Teenage Dragon'.

"Roari, you will never guess what happened last night…"

Whilst he quietly munched on his tea, Imogen told him all about the children from Undurbedd and asked:

"Did you know about the World of Undurbedd?"

They had been friends for 2 years, ever since Imogen had found the stone in the woods. She hadn't known it was magic, but one day when she was holding her stone and had been worried about her friend Susie's lost dog, she had accidentally called Roari from his world. Roari had told her that such stones were very rare. The stone had split into two equal parts when they'd first met and Imogen had given Roari the other half.

Roari had come back to see Imogen many times. Only she could see him, so she wasn't worried her Mum or a neighbour would see them together. She laughed to herself as she thought about trying to explain a 4-metre-high dragon to her Mum!

"Hmmm…", said Roari. "I haven't heard of Undurbedd, but Mum and Dad say there are many lands that are linked together through magic."

He leaned forward and whispered. "I've heard that there is valley over the tall mountains by our cave, that can take you to another world. One day I will take you there and we can explore it together."

He then sat back and said thoughtfully, "I will ask Mum and Dad if they know of Undurbedd."

Roari stretched out and basked in the sun whilst they talked about the Undurbedders. Then Roari yawned and let out a huge plume of dark blue smoke and a tiny flame with it. His time was different to Imogen's world, and sometimes it was day and sometimes night. Strangely, whenever they went off together, they always returned at the same time they left. She liked that because it saved her trying to explain where she had been to her Mum and Dad.

Roari yawned again. "I must go, it's bed time at home." Imogen went over and gave him a hug and as she stood back, warm air started to rush past her, along with a noise like a firework. He had gone.

Imogen smiled and settled back against the shed, pleased to have been able to tell her story to someone and to wonder when she would see the children from Undurbedd again.

Chapter 3 - The Necklace

A month had seemed to race by since Imogen had seen Norti and Corshus. Yet as she snuggled up in bed, in many ways it felt as though it was only yesterday that they had appeared. She felt the bed becoming warmer and softer and her thoughts less joined up.

Then she heard it. The whisper, it was them! She sat up, all thoughts of sleep forgotten, leant over the bed and looked down, her heart pounding. It WAS them! For creeping out and looking carefully around was Corshus. She stopped, as if aware of somebody watching, quickly turned around and stared at Imogen, then grinned as she recognised her friend. Imogen grinned happily in return, but just then Norti followed her out, straining to see behind him and up at the bed and promptly bumped into Corshus.

"Norti! Will you look where you are going!"

Imogen laughed with pleasure. "Are you alright? I didn't think I would see you again, can you stay longer this time?"

"Yes Imogen I am. No thanks to you Norti... again," Corshus replied gruffly.

Before she could speak again Norti blurted out, "We've come to see you because Wilmena has stopped the patrols."

Excited and confused, she looked down at Corshus, who was already scolding Norti.

"Imogen won't know what you are talking about, Norti," and looking up at Imogen she continued, "he's right though, Wilmena the Wise has asked Creagh and all the other Watchers to travel to the Outlands, so there is no one left to guard the doors. We thought it would be safe for us to come back."

Imogen slid off the bed and carefully sat beside them. She was so pleased to see them.

"So how long can you stay this time?"

"We know we can't stay long, because it will give us the sleeping sickness." Norti replied.

"What's the sleeping sickness?"

"It's what happens if you stay here too long, you fall asleep and never wake up. Everyone knows it," replied Corshus. She looked at Norti who nodded seriously back. "It's true," but she hesitated and bit her lip.

"You know when you found my broken necklace, well when we got back, I showed it to Mum and told her we had broken it."

She laughed and said, "Norti is always breaking things so she didn't ask any more. But then Mum and me took it to the metal man…"

"He's very old and has a long white beard!" exclaimed Norti.

"Ssshhh, she's not going to be interested Norti," she said, looking up at Imogen and shaking her head.

"When he looked at it he told Mum that it is a very old necklace and he had heard that many, many years ago it had brought an Ovurbedder to the Land! So, we thought, that if we came to see you, perhaps we could use the necklace to let you come back with us, just for a short time."

They both went quiet and looked at Imogen who was open mouthed with excitement. "What now? But how?"

Corshus reached behind her head, furrowed her brow in concentration and after a while undid the necklace and held it out to Imogen.

She sighed, "I hate undoing it, it's so complicated."

Then she said in a serious but excited tone, "We think..."

But Norti burst out, "if you put on the necklace, it will make you able to come with us, but..." and he wrinkled his face, "we're not sure why or what will happen. I suppose it could go wrong and if you wrapped it around a finger there would be too much magic and it could go black and drop off!"

He smiled, pleased with himself that he had thought of it.

Corshus hit Norti on the shoulder. "Idiot!" she said and stepped up to Imogen and took her fingers between her own hands. Imogen thought Corshus' hands felt so lovely and soft.

"You don't have to come, because we are not really sure how it works. But we do know that the Ovurbedder who visited returned to Ovurbedd. That is what the metal man said."

Imogen thought about what Corshus had said. She felt a bit frightened but then she remembered the warmth of the sun through the door, the richness of the colours and the way everything just looked different. She longed to see the Undurbedd world.

"Let's do it", she whispered excitedly.

Corshus and Norti clasped hands and they all started to talk at once. But then Imogen said, "let me get dressed and we can start."

She got up and put on her jeans and top, whilst Norti looked away and kicked the carpet, which made Corshus and Imogen giggle quietly. Then she knelt down in front of them.

"What do we do now?"

Corshus and Norti grinned and then looked at each other seriously.

Corshus held out her necklace again. "Let me put it on your wrist. Be careful you don't break it…"

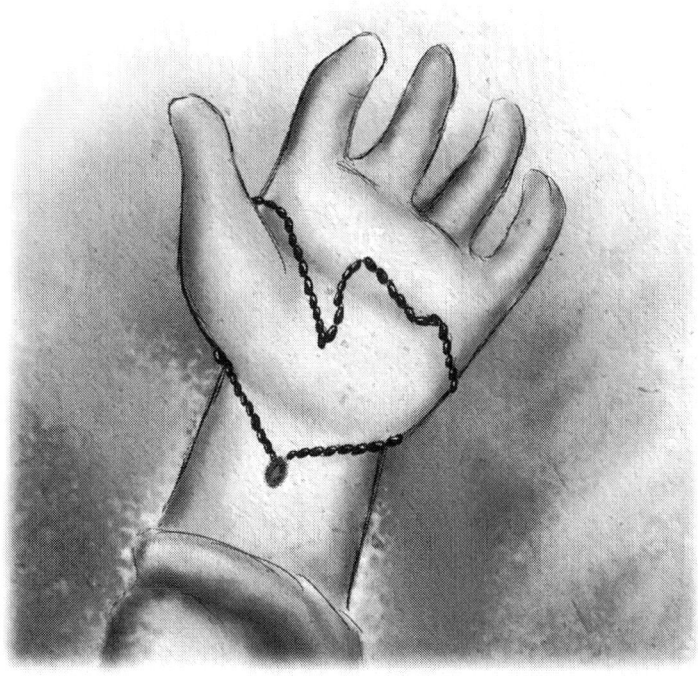

Imogen held out her arm and Corshus wrapped the gold necklace around her wrist and did up the clasp. Fortunately, Imogen had slim wrists so it fitted. She carefully placed the necklace, with the stone facing her, on top of her wrist. It felt warm, not cold against her. Then the stone caught her eye again. She realised one part of it was cloudy and grey. But the rest, maybe two-thirds of it, was clear and shiny. They were all quiet as they watched it.

For a moment nothing happened. Then they all gasped as the central clear stone started to pulse green. It grew brighter and brighter, lighting up all their faces and filling the room with colour. Then when it seemed it could not grow any brighter, it started to pulse even more quickly. Imogen squinted, hardly able to look at the bright pulsing light. Then she gasped. She couldn't believe it. The necklace! It was getting looser on her wrist. It was growing in size!

Still looking at the necklace, she whispered, "Corshus, the necklace, it's getting bigger!" She looked up from her wrist and straight into Corshus' staring eyes. Corshus shook her head silently and then stuttered. "It's... it's you! You are getting smaller!"

Norti nodded vigorously in agreement.

Imogen then realised that Corshus had grown. Norti had as well! But they hadn't. She looked around her. Everything was getting bigger. She was shrinking. The room, the ceiling, the bed beside her were all growing. She wanted to slide the necklace off her wrist, but something held her back. She shrank and shrank until all three were the same size, when the stone completely faded and stopped pulsing. The necklace hung from her wrist.

"What should I do now?" Imogen asked them both. Norti looked at Corshus and with his most thoughtful expression said, "Do you think you should keep the necklace on around your wrist, to stop you growing?"

Corshus raised her eyebrows in surprise and turned to Imogen. "Not like you Norti, but that's a really good idea..."

Corshus slipped off the necklace and tied it around Imogen's wrist, so that it could not fall off. Imogen was so excited.

Norti frowned and said in a thoughtful tone, "I think we had better stay here for a few minutes just to make sure you don't grow back again…" Corshus just stared at him for a moment and then said quietly, "That's a very sensible idea Norti," which made Norti look both pleased and a bit embarrassed.

Imogen agreed because secretly she did wonder what would happen if she started to grow and couldn't get back to her bedroom. She felt this strange mix of excitement and apprehension. But mostly excitement.

Corshus took Imogen's hand in hers and looking at her steadily said, "I'm sure that if it didn't happen when the Ovurbedder visited all those years ago, it should be okay now. Why else would it have stopped when you shrunk to our size. It must know somehow."

Imogen nodded but wasn't completely sure, nor even that Corshus fully believed what she was saying.

They all sat down and talked about other things to stop worrying. They concentrated on what they should do when they got there. Norti wanted to go to their home, but Corshus wasn't sure about what either of their parents would say. They decided they would take her to the area near the river, which was close by their home, so she could see where they went after school.

Behind them, in the wall, at the far end of the bed and framed by light was the open door. The door to Undurbedd. They kept looking at it whilst talking about where they would go and what Imogen would see, but all the time they could feel it pulling them towards it.

Imogen then said, "Are you two brother and sister?"

Norti screwed up his face and Corshus looked shocked.

"No!" they said at the same time.

Norti was especially put out. "Her, my sister? No way!"

Corshus shook her head and said, "No, but we have known each other all our lives. Our parents live next door to each other."

They all went quiet. "I'm nervous, are you?" asked Imogen. The other two both nodded. Then Corshus took Imogen's hand, looked her and just said, "Now?"

Imogen nodded and together, hearts pounding, the three of them held hands and walked towards the door in the wall.

Chapter 4 – Undurbedd

Norti and Corshus picked up their backpacks as they moved towards the door in the wall. In the half light of the moon, Imogen decided they did not look like her own backpack. In fact, theirs looked like giant leaves sewn together. The shoulder straps looked like big pieces of grass, shiny and a deep green. They also looked full and she wondered what was inside.

Norti reached the door first. Imogen was able to see it properly for the first time. It was dark brown and old. The hinges were big and square and spread out across half of the door. They were held onto the door by metal studs, each with a small rune, carved into the top of the stud. Norti pulled on the ancient looking metal handle. The door groaned open and light and warmth flooded in. Imogen held her breath as a world of green was revealed.

They stepped through and she felt the turf beneath her feet. It felt so soft, and spongy beneath her feet. She loved the way the grass tickled her between her toes.

Corshus smiled at Imogen. "Here, only grown-ups wear shoes, because of their work, but we don't."

She laughed and wiggled her fawn coloured toes. Imogen thought they looked more like paws than toes. She smelt the grass and flowers and something else, she didn't know what. It just made her want to drink it in and smile and laugh. It was wonderful. She felt nervous and shy of moving too far but at the same time, so full of joy that she wanted to run and run and run.

In front of her were gentle rolling fields of green grass but with clumps of trees and huge bushes. Some had large, silver teardrop shapes dripping down from the thick bush branches. The tears were as big as she was and seemed to be made of a silky, shimmery material. But they were high above her head, so she couldn't touch them to find out.

There were banks of flowers everywhere, mixes of reds and yellows and blues. They were like the flowers at home but different. There were daffodils similar to the ones at home, but they were blue. The centre of the flowers were shiny and gold, like brass trumpets. Yet they were as soft and delicate as any petal of any flower and were also as tall as her chest.

"This way!" shouted Norti, who started to run down the field towards a slow-moving river, that was so blue in colour it looked like the sky. Corshus took Imogen's hand and together they ran after Norti until all three were by the river bank. The water was still a deep blue so she couldn't see the bottom or if there were any fish. Just as Imogen was wondering if she could drink it, Norti dropped to his knees, scooped out a handful of water and drank deeply. Corshus followed suit and they both looked at Imogen with a puzzled look.

"Is there something wrong?" Corshus asked.

"I've never drunk blue water before." Imogen said shyly.

Then as they watched her, she bent down and cupping her hand, lifted a little water to her lips. It didn't smell bad and thinking 'here goes' she sipped it. It tasted lovely. In fact it was the sweetest and best water she had ever drank, so she quickly scooped up some more. Just then a fish as long as her arm jumped out of the water, caught a fly hovering above it and fell back in. She stood watching and sure enough another one jumped out, its silver and blue body flashing in the sunlight. They both laughed at her and then Norti pronounced, "I'm hungry."

He promptly reached into his backpack and pulled out what looked like a coil of something. The end was a handle, which looked like a stiff rope or even wood. It didn't make sense to Imogen.

Whilst Corshus busied herself making a fire near the river bank, Norti held the end of the coil tightly in his hand and then holding the handle, held it out at arm's length towards the water. It immediately sprang out over the water until it was straight. Then with a flick of his wrist it came back into a coil, which Norti held in his hand again. It was a bit like a fishing rod, Imogen thought.

With his rod firmly held in his arm, he went to the water's edge and waited. Suddenly a fish leapt.

Norti instantly held out his arm as though pointing at the fish. The coil leapt out at the fish, its thin end wrapped around it. Norti jerked it onto the river bank.

In the next few minutes, the flames from the fire and the pile of fish grew. Imogen watched in fascination as Corshus cleaned the fish and started to roast them over the fire with sticks she had pulled out from the backpack. They seemed to be sticks of wood but didn't burn. But then she thought, everything looked nearly the same as at home and then turn out to be, well, just different.

"Imogen...Imogen..." Norti was calling her from her thoughts.

"Here," he said a little impatiently and on a plate was salad of some sort, a beautifully cooked fish and a silver coloured fork with two prongs. The meal tasted even better than it looked. The fish melted in her mouth and was full of the loveliest and most delicate flavours.

The salad was a mixture of greens and reds and blues. It was soft and melted on her tongue. They all quickly finished their fish and reached for more. For 20 minutes there was silence, until they sat back with full tummies and sighed in contentment.

Imogen lay back on the soft, green grass and noticed that it smells just like newly cut grass at home but more so, even though it hadn't been cut!

She gathered up the plates and swilled them clean in the river. When she was done, Imogen stood up and looked at the river.

"It looks so nice. Do you swim in it?"

"Of course, all the time," said Norti, "perhaps next time…" he stopped and looked at Corshus and shyly added, "if you would like to come back and the Watchers are still away, we could all go swimming!"

"Oh yes, that would be great."

"Shall we explore a bit, Imogen? I'm sure it will be safe," said Corshus.

So together they started off along the riverbank, watching the fish jump out of the water. Corshus and Norti took turns explaining how a certain bed of flowers was a great place to hide and which were the best climbing bushes and which had the tastiest fruit and who preferred which bush best. Corshus was laughing or scolding Norti not to exaggerate. At that point Norti declared he had climbed to the top of the slim tomato bush, even though it was 20 meters high.

"Now that is true," said Corshus and smiled at them both, "it swayed around as he neared the top, far too much for me!"

"What about the trees, don't you climb them?" Imogen asked.

Corshus carefully and seriously explained that they didn't climb the trees, because they were the homes of birds and it was against The Book of Words to disturb their homes. They weren't quite sure why, just that they mustn't.

"What are the big silver things in the bushes in the distance?" Imogen pointed to her left and up the hill. They were the same silver things she had briefly seen in the distance when Corshus and Norti had last visited her.

"We sleep in them," said Norti, "I can't see how you sleep on that big flat thing you lie on."

"It's what you're used to Norti," said Corshus, "we are just used to different things. The same as we are all used to you breaking things."

"Just because Mum said it once... and the necklace wasn't my fault..."

But Imogen had stopped listening. She was enjoying the rich, sweet scent of the roses. The roses were 2 metres tall and each stem was as thick as her wrist and grew straight up, with one large, wide leaf on each side. On top of each stem was a single flower the size of soup plate. A rose of many petals. There were reds and yellows and they all swayed in the wind. It reminded her of the fields of maize the farmer at home was growing.

Just then, the ground started to rumble. Corshus and Norti both gasped. "Watchers!" they said together and each grabbed one of Imogen's hand. Before she could say anything, they were pulling her as fast as they could towards the rose forest.

Chapter 5 - The Watchers

They rushed into the forest, hearts pounding, the large leaves slapping their faces. They only stopped to turn around once they were sure they were deep enough not to be seen. They huddled beside each other, felt the ground rumble louder, gripping each other's hands.

Imogen was frightened because she could see how worried the other two were.

"What is it? Why are we hiding?" she gasped, still breathless.

"Shush!" hissed Norti and gradually they eased back nearer to the forest edge, so they could see safely. "Why have you stopped, Creagh?" said one of the Watchers, in a voice you didn't argue with. "My mount, he's nervous, aren't you boy. Must have seen or smelt something unusual," said another. "Well we don't have time to wait, we must report back to Wilmena before the sun sets…"

Imogen had crept very quietly, but not as quietly as the children, towards the voices. Corshus turned around and put a finger to her mouth and signalled she must stop where she was, a few metres behind them. The big leaves meant she couldn't see who or what was talking. Despite her nerves, she stopped behind them to see what was happening. Being as careful as she could, she stepped up to the

crouching children and gave a sudden gasp, for side on and near the forest edge was a rider, one of many.

She was tall, with large-brown eyes, eyes that were constantly on the move watching. She was dressed in a green cap that covered the back of her ears, a green tunic that looked like it was made of leather but had leaf veins in it. Her leggings were soft and brown in colour, like her thin shoes.

The stranger was riding a fox. She thought the animal had to be 2 metres high. Its fur was luxuriant, and rich red, all the way to end of its long tail. Its eyes looked watchful and almost angry, constantly looking around it. It had no bridle or bit and Imogen realised its rider was controlling it with her legs, only occasionally leaning forward to stroke its head and calm it.

"I'm sure there is something unusual here, I can feel it," said Creagh in an irritable tone.

"Well, we cannot continue to wait. Stay and check if you wish, we must away." She turned around to the other Watchers and addressed them.

"Watchers forward."

Her fox sprang forward and was followed by a long line of other riders.

The children felt the ground tremble as the animals sped away, but they were so fast they quickly started to disappear. Creagh was clearly torn, looking around and then at the disappearing figures, working with his knees to control his mount. His fox wanted to follow the others.

"Come my beauty, you are right, we must catch up." His mount sprang forward and in a matter of seconds they were gone.

Corshus and Norti looked at each other and let their foreheads touch for a second.

"That was close Corshus. Think what would have happened if they had found us." Norti had a serious expression on his face. This was a new Norti that Imogen hadn't seen before.

"Are they the Watchers that stop you coming to my world?"

They nodded silently, then Corshus spoke.

"We didn't expect them back. They watch the doors, not only to stop us going to Ovurbedd, but to stop Ovurbedders coming here. We don't know what they would do if they found you, especially as Wilmena the Wise has not invited you. The one giving orders was Leadser. She is the chief Watcher We thought they were to be gone for days, you see."

Norti came to Corshus' defence. "Her Mum said that, because her Dad is a watcher."

He stopped and bit his lip. "I'm sorry Imogen, this is all my fault, I persuaded Corshus to bring you, she was against it."

"Should I be scared?" said Imogen, feeling very scared and a bit cross.

Norti spoke, frowning and looking between the two others. "We don't know, but we had better get you back without you being seen. We can do that, can't we Corshus?"

"Ofcourse we can," she said, not sounding as convinced as she wanted to.

Imogen started to speak but stopped. She wanted to be angry, but she knew it was her choice to come. She took a deep breath.

"Do we go now or wait for a bit?"

Corshus nodded and said, "I think we should try and get as close to the door as we can and then decide when to go through it."

Norti immediately agreed. "Yes, I think we can go now, because Leadser, head of the Watchers, said she wanted to see Wilmena. They are all gathering by the Speaking Hall."

Corshus and Norti stood holding hands, almost back to back. Imogen could see them sniffing the air, their ears twitching. Their eyes were constantly looking for any movement.

"Is it safe?" she said.

"Shush!" said Norti, as they looked and listened. Then after a moment, Norti turned to Imogen, "yes it's safe to move."

They quietly stepped out of the forest, looking all around them and then hurried as fast as they could from bush to tree to flower to forest of roses, retracing their steps. Imogen's heart was pounding and she felt sick. She didn't look at any of the strange trees or bushes or the food hanging down from them. She had no appetite or interest. All she could do was concentrate on looking out for the Watchers and willing the Hill of Doors to get closer.

The journey seemed to take forever, with the sun dropping further and further towards the horizon. From the corner of her eye, every long evening shadow looked like a Watcher. They followed the river around a long curve that Imogen hadn't noticed earlier and there in the distance was the endless line of doors and hills, disappearing into the evening mist. Imogen was so relieved that the end of this horrible journey was in sight. Norti suddenly stopped, grabbed their hands and scuttled behind a large tree trunk.

There, up the short hill to the doors was a Watcher, crouching down outside a door. He was examining the grass, pulled some up and sniffed it. He had a puzzled expression on his face. "It's Creagh, Imogen," hissed Norti, "it's Creagh kneeling beside your door!"

Norti turned to Corshus. "What shall we do? We can't get Imogen past him."

But the Watcher must have heard something, because at that moment he looked up and around and seeing Norti peering around the tree trunk, called out, "Norti, is that you? Come here boy and now!" It was definitely Creagh.

Norti left the cover of the tree and walked towards Creagh. Corshus hadn't seen him and was startled when she heard Creagh speak. She quickly turned and looking worried took Imogen's hand. Imogen was suddenly very afraid.

As Norti slowly walked towards him, Creagh said, "I have no idea why you are here, we'll talk about that later. I need you to stay here and watch. If any strangers pass by or go through one of the doors, note the door and go to Leadser, she should be with Wilmena. I need to follow these tracks."

He stopped, looked at Norti for a second and said questioningly, "You don't know anything about these tracks, do you?"

Norti froze, but before he could speak Creagh continued, "Of course you don't. Do you understand what I have told you? Well speak up, do you understand?"

"Yes Watcher, I understand. If I see a stranger go through a door I am to go to Leadser and tell her." Creagh shook his head. "And don't forget to note which door. Norti, I do wonder about you boy. Put this dagger in the ground in front of it, in case you forget the name on the door. Try not to cut yourself on it."

Still shaking his head, he knelt down and started to follow the tracks they had made when they had first arrived, the tracks that led to the riverbank where they had stopped for lunch. The tracks which went past the very tree Corshus and Imogen were hiding behind.

Norti stood stock still. 'Corshus must be warned somehow,' he thought. He shouted out, "Don't worry Creagh, I will stay here whilst you go towards the river."

Creagh turned around, frowned, started to walk back towards Norti, then shook his head and continued to follow the tracks slowly down towards the river.

Norti held his breath as Creagh moved towards the tree, head down so he could still make out the three sets of tracks, the two normal ones and the one with the strangely long and unusual footprint. Corshus had heard Norti's shout and immediately understood what he was really saying. Putting her finger to her mouth she quickly motioned to Imogen that Creagh was going to come past the tree where they were hiding. She signalled that they needed to go around the tree, as he went past, to keep out of sight.

"Which side?" Imogen signalled back.

Corshus looked straight into her eyes and with a worried look, shrugged her shoulders. Norti watched Creagh get nearer and nearer the tree. It was big, so he wouldn't have seen them yet. But he knew Creagh was bound to see them if they didn't move around the tree, as he went past it.

As he got closer to the tree, Norti cried out in a puzzled tone, "Creagh!"

"What now?" he retorted without slowing or looking back. "Well, what do you want?" Clearly annoyed, he kept following the tracks to the left of the tree.

It had been enough. Creagh's voice told Corshus which side of the tree he was coming around. She took Imogen by the arm and with Imogen against her front, she gradually eased her round the tree. Imogen carefully shuffled forward. She felt Corshus' fingers dig into her arm and could hear her short breaths. She could hardly breathe herself and her heart was pounding.

Imogen thought to herself, 'what if they find me, what will they do? Will they keep me? What about Mum and Dad?'

They shuffled further round the tree. Suddenly, all thoughts went. In front of them and looking down at the ground was Creagh. Imogen froze, her heart in her mouth. She couldn't move or think. She felt Corshus bump into her and give a quiet gasp. Nobody moved. He looked so big and menacing as he stared at the ground. Imogen was sure she could hear him growling. She knew he would see them at any second. Imogen felt her heart pound, she was sure he would hear!

Norti was staring down at them open mouthed. Creagh was bound to see them. "Sorry Watcher, didn't mean to disturb you. It's nothing, it can wait."

For a moment there was silence and no movement. Creagh cursed under his breath and turned back towards Norti, but away from the tree and Imogen. He hadn't seen them!

"Boy, I need to follow these tracks before darkness. If I can't follow them because you have held me up, I shall come back for you! Understand? Idiot boy!"

He spun around on his heel, just as Imogen and Corshus shuffled back behind the tree away from him. Continuing to mutter, Creagh walked back to the spot on the ground, where he had been staring and then quickly moved away from the tree, following the three sets of tracks that Imogen and the others had made when they strolled down to the river.

Imogen and Corshus held on to each other tightly and watched his back as he walked away. Imogen pulled Corshus away, so Creagh wouldn't see them if he turned back. They waited for Norti to signal the all clear.

For what seemed an age to Imogen, Norti stood still, staring at Creagh's disappearing back. When he was finally out of sight, she saw Norti sink to the ground in sheer relief. Getting back up, he waved to them to come up the hill and as soon as Imogen and Corshus arrived, they held each other's shaking hands and together they ran towards Imogen's door.

There, the three of them hugged each other out of excitement, relief, but also fear that they could still be caught.

Opening the door, Norti whispered urgently, "Quickly, Imogen." And with a final hug and kiss to both of them, she was through.

"Don't forget me," Imogen whispered to them as the door started to close.

"The necklace!" shouted Corshus through the closing door. "You must let me undo the necklace.

Only Mum and I can undo it. We will have to come with you…"

Corshus pushed the door back, and leaving it slightly ajar, she took Imogen's hands and then all three ran under the bed and into the bedroom. Imogen turned around to face Corshus, who took the necklace and tried to undo it. She tried again and again, but she couldn't get it to open. Norti was getting anxious and kept looking back at the open door.

"Hurry up," he hissed, "Creagh could come back and shut the door."

"I know. Shut up Norti, I have to concentrate. The clasp has to be pressed in a special way." Corshus stopped, took a deep breath and slowly pressed the clasp three times. It sprang open.

All three grinned. The necklace slid from Imogen's wrist. She held out the necklace, with the stone facing her. They stood still watching, first the stone and then Imogen. Nothing was happening. Imogen kept looking at Corshus' eyes to see if she was getting smaller. Nothing.

Then suddenly the stone began to change colour. It became paler and then white and grew brighter and brighter. Imogen was staring so hard she forgot to look at Corshus, but the light was becoming blinding to look at. She looked away and then at Corshus, who along with Norti was looking away from the blinding light. She was looking down at Corshus. She was growing. She grinned and laughed. She was returning to her proper height. The others looked up at her and grinned in return.

"I'm growing," she laughed and took a step back so she wouldn't tread on her friends.

"I was getting worried," said Norti, "I mean, what would have happened if you hadn't grown?"

"Oh, shut up Norti!" said Corshus, "we can all relax now."

"What about Creagh? He might be out there waiting for us," said Norti, remembering how he had been threatened. Then, seeing that the stone's colour was turning pale and then dying, he added, "We had better go before anything else happens." Corshus smiled up at Imogen. "Have you grown to your normal height? Because if so, Norti is right, we had better go."

Imogen looked around. She felt she was the right height. She looked down. "Yes, everything feels fine." She smiled and bent down and held out two fingers which they both took between their hands. They smiled up at Imogen, then at each other and without another word quickly ran towards the bed and door.

"Good bye Imogen!" they called out as they ran.

Imogen knelt down and watched them rush to the door. She whispered "goodbye" as they went through it and shut the door behind them.

This time she stayed and watched as the door first became fuzzy in outline and then change colour to the cream of the wall, before slowly disappearing. No trace was left. After a few seconds, she wasn't even sure, exactly where the door had been. She stood up, feeling tired and sat on the bed. She took a sip of water from her glass on the bedside table. She pulled a face because it suddenly tasted very ordinary and almost bitter, compared to the river water of Undurbedd.

She smiled at the memory of her day, the excitement, and less about the frightening bits. She felt herself grow tired again and let herself fall into bed. She was so sleepy. She idly thought it was strange that it was still night time at home. She couldn't ask her Mum or Dad, but maybe Roari would know.

Chapter 6:
Imogen and Roari make a plan

"Imogen, sweetheart, it's time to wake up. You are a sleepy head today." She felt her Mum's hand in her hair. "It is a mass of curls today. Didn't you brush your hair last night? It's got bits of grass in it."

Mum frowned slightly and with a look of concentration took them carefully out of her hair.

"I don't remember them there last night, what were you and your friend Susie doing in the garden yesterday?"

Imogen was instantly awake. She looked up at her Mum and didn't know what to say. But before she could speak her Mum shrugged her shoulders, smiled, kissed her forehead. "Well it's late and breakfast is ready, so up you get and come straight down."

Before Imogen could say a word, she had left the room and headed down the stairs. She raced up out of bed and checked her hair in the mirror. Her Mum was right, there were bits of grass in her hair. She checked her clothes. They had bits of twig and grass on them as well. There was even a small piece of a petal. She looked at the bit of petal and thought how strange it was that the bits of twig and petal had grown as well.

She wondered if Roari would know. She started to remember the mixture of excitement, of being in a different world and then remembering how frightening it had become when her Mum called up. "Breakfast is on the table and getting cold!" "Coming, Mum!" she called back and raced for the stairs.

Mum was busy tidying up. She needed to work at home today. Dad had gone to visit Grandad to help mend his fence, so Imogen would be on her own. Imogen said that she would be fine and be in the back garden.

Later that morning, Dad set out to Granddad's and Mum said she wanted to tidy up her desk and wasn't to be disturbed. Imogen would normally be a bit sad that she was left on her own on a Sunday, but today she smiled inside with pleasure.

"Okay Mum, I'll be in the garden," and whilst excited inside, tried to go out in an unhurried fashion. Once outside though, she ran to the back of the shed and, holding her stone, called Roari.

She grinned as he appeared. Roari stretched out his long wings and shook himself all over. He turned to her, "That's better," he said. "Do you want to go out today?"

"Oh Roari," she exclaimed. "I have so much to tell you! I have been to their world. I've been to Undurbedd!"

Without stopping, she told him all about her adventure there.

Roari lay down and quietly listened until she breathlessly came to the end of her story. "That's amazing Imogen, but..." and putting his head to one side, "it could have been dangerous. I asked Mum and Dad about Undurbedd and they said they don't like people from other lands. Even dragons aren't welcome. Dad said they had a calling stone, but he thinks it is much bigger and more powerful than any other one. He said he didn't know how, but it stops anyone from another world entering it unless they are invited."

He stopped and became more thoughtful. As did Imogen.

"So how was it so easy for me to enter Undurbedd then?" she asked.

"I don't know. I will ask Dad, but you must be careful. Promise me either not to go back, or if you do, to take the calling stone. Because if you can go there, it probably means I can. Do you promise?"

Imogen had never seen Roari serious like this before and realised she needed to think carefully about going back. She remembered how frightened she had been in the rose wood and when Creagh was hunting them. But then she sighed because she also knew how excited she had been in the new land and how much fun she had had with Corshus and Norti. But she also remembered how worried they had been about going back to their village.

"I promise Roari. I can't see me going back there. It was so lovely though," she added wistfully.

It was getting near lunchtime and she thought her Mum would be looking for her, so they said goodbye and Roari disappeared back to his world. Imogen ran up the garden, pleased that she had been able to tell Roari about her adventure. She happily went to bed early because she was still tired after the previous night. She wondered if she would see the Undurbedders again, but drifted off to sleep before she could think anymore.

The next day she was so tired that she was in bed early again. Somehow she wasn't sleepy though. She wondered again about what Roari had said and what she should do if they came back. She sighed because she didn't know what to do if they came back. But then it seemed unlikely.

"Imogen...Imogen..." Louder this time. She came out of a deep sleep and knew instantly it was Corshus. She leant over the bed and there they were.

She felt overjoyed, Corshus was safe.

"I've been worried about you Corshus. Did Creagh find you? Did you get into trouble?"

Corshus smiled back, but it was serious smile. "Yes, he did."

Imogen gasped and put her hands to her mouth, then quickly got off the bed and sat down and looking at them both, whispered, "What happened? Are you alright?"

"You tell her," said Norti, but looking up at Imogen he added, "we don't have much time."

They sat down in front of her and Corshus put her hand on Imogen's knee.

"We are here to tell you what happened, but also to ask you to come back with us. Wilmena the Wise knows about you and wishes to speak to you. She promises that you will be welcome and safe."

Imogen just nodded, she didn't know what to say or think.

Corshus took a deep breath and explained. "When we shut the doorway, Creagh was there waiting for us. It had got too dark for him to follow our trail and he had come back to fetch Norti and his knife." Corshus' head dropped.

"He was very angry," she said simply, "he marched us back to the village and took us to Wilmena." She bit her lip. "She was lying down, she is very ill. Do you remember Leadser?" Imogen nodded.

"Well she was there with the other Watchers and so were our Dads. Everyone stopped talking when we came in. Then Creagh told them how he had found us and everyone went really quiet and then they all started talking and our Dads were shouting." Norti burst out. "They were all so cross with us, they all shouted at once at us, including Dad. It was horrible, wasn't it Corshus?"

She nodded her head in agreement, but she was grim-faced remembering it.

"We were scared what was going to happen. But Wilmena didn't speak. She just stared and then she sat up and beckoned us to come forward and then for everyone to be quiet. She just kept looking at us from top to bottom. We wondered what she was looking at. Then Wilmena said, 'Who did you bring here child?'

Corshus continued, her face full of concern, "We had to tell her about you, Imogen, you do understand, don't you?"

Imogen just nodded in agreement. She didn't know what to say.

Corshus dropped her voice to almost a whisper. "Then she touched me, stroked my tunic and looked at her hands. Then she took my shoulders and looked into my eyes and said, 'for the sake of this Land, for all our sakes, you must fetch her, this Imogen. I promise you'. Then Wilmena looked at the Watchers around us, and continued, 'we all promise you that she shall be safe here. But you must fetch her tomorrow. Will you do this? For me. For all of us.'"

Corshus looked at Norti, who nodded in agreement. "The others started to protest and ask her why she was saying this, but she just held up her hand and said, 'all will be understood when the time is right'. So we had to promise her, and that's why we are here."

Corshus looked into Imogen's eyes. "Will you come?"

Imogen wanted to hug her, hug them both. She was nervous but excited all in one. She bit her lip. She remembered what Roari had had said and what she had promised him. But this was different.

Neither she or Roari had expected this. She looked at them both.

"Do you think I will be okay if I come back with you?"

They both nodded earnestly. "Wilmena could never lie," said Norti.

Imogen looked at them, then feeling both nervous and excited, she nodded, grinned and nodded again. "Yes. I'll come. Let me get dressed."

She quickly got up from the floor and got ready. She was just about to put her hand out for the necklace, when she remembered what Roari said. She picked up her stone from beside the pillow.

She knelt down and as before, after Corshus laid the necklace across her wrist, she watched for the stone to change colour. All too quickly she had shrunk to the Undurbedders' size and all three were running towards the open door.

Chapter 7 - Wilmena explains all

Corshus opened the door and as the light flooded through Imogen gasped, because there, looking down at her, eyes angry, mistrustful and arms crossed, was Creagh.

"I don't know why Wilmena has summoned you, but never forget, you are a stranger here and strangers are not welcome. I will be watching you."

Imogen stood back and didn't know what to say, But Norti and Corshus stood as one between Imogen and Creagh. Norti looked up defiantly.

"Wilmena promised she would be safe didn't she?" He glared at them all and then turned on his heel.

"Quickly," he snarled, "hurry, you are wasting my time," and started to walk towards his mount. There were two smaller foxes waiting for them.

Corshus took Imogen's hand. "He's always like this. You are safe here. No one in the village will go against Wilmena's word. Come on," she said and seeing Imogen looking at the foxes, added, "you are to sit behind me."

Imogen looked up at the fox. Fortunately, she knew how to ride a horse, but she was sure riding a giant fox would be very different. Corshus quickly mounted with Norti's help and he then helped Imogen up behind her. Creagh yelled a command and all three foxes sprang forward, Norti and Corshus following him.

Imogen held on as the fox gained speed. The land looked different sitting behind Corshus, but she didn't have time to look around. She concentrated on holding on and trying to adjust to the fox's movement. It felt strange, there were no hoof noises but silence as the foxes' pads brushed the ground.

All too soon the village came into view. She could see more clearly this time that it was a series of different sized bushes. They were the size of a large oak or chestnut trees back home. In between some of the bushes were cone-shaped tents.

Corshus explained that the tents were used as workplaces, whereas the bushes were mostly for living and sleeping. The closer they got, she began to realise how little she had seen the first time and how large the village was. It seemed to stretch on for some distance. Corshus said that it had many hundreds of people, but she didn't know how many exactly, no one had ever counted.

They slowed as they entered the outskirts and Imogen saw people noticing the three foxes and their riders. She felt very shy and nervous as the villagers realised Corshus had a stranger behind her. They began coming down from the bushes or from the sleeping pods, or standing up from small gatherings around cooking fires to stare.

The villagers went quiet as they stopped and stared at Imogen. Some with a smile of welcome or sympathy, some with puzzlement, but others with frowns. Many were dressed in all the colours of the flowers that she had seen on her first visit. Trousers and tunics of every colour. Even their caps were petals, the many different colours sewn together.

But others wore the brown that Leadser and the Watchers wore.

Gradually they made their way through the people. Imogen noticed the initial quiet was replaced by murmurs of conversation.

Followed by the villagers, they made their way through the village into a large central square, that was dominated by the biggest of all bushes. It was dome shaped, but she couldn't make out any branches because the leaves were so large and overlapped each other, forming a perfect covering that stretched to the ground. Creagh halted his steed and signalled for the others to do so. They were quickly surrounded and Imogen didn't know where to look, as all eyes were upon her.

"Welcome, child," croaked a voice from the back. The villagers stepped to one side to reveal a very elderly lady of Undurbedd. She looked very frail and thin, her fur was pale and blotchy, her ears hung low and she leaned heavily on a thin stick that looked as though it was cut from a rose stem.

"Welcome again. Come here, into the Speaking Hall."

Imogen felt Corshus gently push her forward and they followed the lady past the quiet and watchful villagers, towards an opening in the largest bush. She realised that the large bush behind the Lady was like a giant cavern. The inside branches had been cut down, leaving a circular dome of branches and leaves that dropped down to the floor to protect them from the sun and rain. On the floor were carpets of green reeds with leaves. Wooden chairs were facing the far end. Lamps on tall stands were spread throughout the hall, which left only the top of the dome in shadow.

At the far end was a low and wide bed, covered in some sort of the faint rose petals. She sat and then half lay on it, supported by pillows. "Come here child and stand beside me, so I may see you properly."

Imogen quickly looked at Corshus who nodded and signalled with her eyes that she should do as she was asked. This, she realised, was the Lady the others had talked about.

"My name is Wilmena. Wilmena the Wise is my full name." She half-smiled and her eyes laughed, showing that she didn't take the full title too seriously.

"I guide and lead the people of the Land. What is your name?"

"Please, my name is Imogen."

'Well Imogen your young friends, Corshus and Norti, tell me that you are from the other world that we call Ovurbedd. Is that true?"

"Yes, I am," she answered quietly.

Imogen felt so nervous that she didn't say anything except answer the questions with as few words as possible. She was really wishing she was at home with her Mum. Wilmena leant forward and looked at her all over, as if looking for something. Then she seemed to smile and nod to herself, satisfied, and as though she had decided something.

"Child, our land is protected by a stone from strangers who wish us harm and war. It keeps all those who would do us ill at bay and gives the Wise One of the Land the power to rule and heal. This stone is kept by the Wise One and so at this time, by me. This is how it is and how it has been in all the time of our people. But now the stone has been taken without consent by my younger sister. We believe she has gone with it to the outer edges of the Land, where travel is difficult and hiding places abound. She is called Bagsheela. We believe she has taken it for her own use. We think she hopes to bend its power to make herself immortal and rule over the Land. But the stone is resisting this corruption of its power. I fear it or indeed the very Land may be destroyed or weakened beyond measure. It is already weakening me. I fear I will not live many days."

Imogen listened intently, too fearful and upset to move a muscle or speak. She wondered at the story and how it involved her. She waited for Wilmena to gather herself before continuing. Wilmena's breathing steadied and she smiled at Imogen.

"When your young friends were brought to me last night," she nodded in Corshus and Norti's direction, "I saw their clothing was covered with green glitter. It was not of this world. It must have come from you. But I see that it is also on you, not part of you. It is a glitter that comes from a creature of power and magic. You know of such a creature, don't you child?"

Imogen nodded. She could only nod, as she became increasingly conscious of the depth of Wilmena's hypnotically deep and liquid brown eyes.

There was a murmur of astonishment from all those that had gathered in the hall. Corshus and Norti were looking increasingly puzzled and were looking at themselves and each other for signs of the glitter. Their gaze constantly moved from Imogen to each other and back again. Wilmena held up her hand and the murmur of conversation quietened and died. She addressed the crowd.

"Only I can see the glitter, it is not visible to anyone who does not control the stone," she looked back at Imogen, "tell me about the creature child."

Imogen struggled to begin, she was so nervous and there were so many people. Wilmena sensed it and looking up, asked all except the Leadser, a few of her Watchers and the children to leave.

When they had gone, the remaining dozen or so people looked at Imogen. The Watchers without emotion, but both Leadser and Wilmena smiled with encouragement. She knew she had to tell the truth, but she also felt that no one wished her or Roari harm. She was sure of it.

Imogen whispered, "He's a dragon and his name is Roari."

This brought a gasp from everyone, except Wilmena. She smiled and nodded her encouragement. "How does he come to you child?"

"I have a stone, it's a 'calling' stone and when I say his name, Roari appears."

"And does he always come when you ask?"

"Yes."

Wilmena smiled and seemed to relax. "Good, that is very good."

She seemed deep in thought for a second. She then sat up and leaned forward and took Imogen's hands in hers. Unlike Corshus, her fur felt dry and harsh, like straw. "Do you have the stone with you?"

Imogen felt frightened for Roari for a second, but the eyes that looked at and into her were kindly and wise. She knew she could not deny Wilmena, but she also felt she could trust her and did not need to be afraid. In fact, she wanted to tell Wilmena all about Roari.

She gave a little smile. "Yes, I have it," and without thinking, pulled out the stone and showed it to Wilmena.

The Watchers and children gasped and Creagh stood up. He pointed at Imogen and shouted, "it's like our stone! Just smaller. It must belong here. She is not to be trusted!"

Imogen gasped and said defiantly, "no it's mine, I brought it with me."

"Fool," cried Wilmena to Creagh, "sit down."

She again held Imogen's hand. "I know it is your stone, it is not whole and has the glitter of the other world deep inside it."

Imogen didn't really understand what Wilmena had said, but somehow was reassured. Just for a moment though, she wondered why Creagh was so angry with her.

Wilmena continued. "I am glad you have brought the stone, for by doing so, you may be the saviour of our land. For I need you..." she took another steadying breath, "for I need you to call your dragon here."

Chapter 8 - Roari is called

Imogen looked at Wilmena open mouthed. "But why? How can Roari help?"

Wilmena smiled in frustration. "Our stone is locked away. It was over a week before I discovered our stone had gone and that it was my own sister, Bagsheela, who along with some 10 Followers had taken it. I sent the Watchers out to try and track them. Sadly, the trail was cold and the outlying areas are rocky and heavily wooded. It is a place to hide a thousand Followers from a thousand Watchers. They continue to look, but I fear Bagsheela will not be found. But it is time that is our enemy. I can feel her warping the way of the stone already. I do not think we have much time before she hurts the Land itself."

Wilmena looked tired but continued.

"We will not find them in time, but your dragon! Your dragon can fly and perhaps could look down and come upon them."

She started to cough and Leadser spoke up.

"I am placing cohorts of Watchers along the darker forest edges, so if Roari finds Bagsheela, he can alert the nearest cohort to rescue the stone and capture her."

Leadser looked grim as she whispered, "Never in our history has someone taken that which was not offered."

Imogen looked at her. "No one steals?"

Leadser looked quizzical, "what is 'steals'?" Then she looked back at Wilmena, who was now lying back against the pillows and staring up urgently at Imogen.

"Child, we need to know, will you call Roari and ask him to help us?"

She need not hesitate, she was sure he would come. It was to help others. And he had already said he would come if she needed his help whilst in the Land.

"Yes of course. But I had better be outside, I'm not sure he would fit in here", she said looking around the bush hall. "Can I call him in private? So I can talk to him first."

"Are we not to be trusted then?" said Creagh. Wilmena just glared at Creagh, who immediately looked down and away. She looked back at Imogen and gently smiled at her.

"Of course, take her to the rear of this hall and there she is to be left alone so that she may call him." Imogen was quickly led from the hall and leaving Corshus at the front, she made her way to the rear of the giant bush.

Alone, she sat down as though she was behind her own garden shed and taking out her half of the calling stone, she whispered his name.

For a few seconds nothing seemed to happen. It felt like an eternity. Then she felt the air change. It became still and warmer and then she felt a rush of air sweeping by her and there was a flash of light and there before her stood Roari.

He was on his back legs and immediately looking around, mouth curled as he made a quiet but threatening deep-throated roar. Smoke and flame seeped out from his mouth. She was shocked because he was clearly ready to defend her. It made her feel a bit guilty that she hadn't thought that such an urgent 'calling' from a new place would worry him.

Imogen jumped up and quickly said, "I'm safe Roari, no one is threatening me, I need you to help the Undurbedders."

She took his arm to reassure him. He kept looking around for a few seconds and then relaxed and looked down at her.

"You worry me. I thought you might be here. My family wondered whether we should all come. But I said, I didn't feel any fear in the call. So, what has happened to bring you back here?"

Imogen quickly explained. She had never seen him look so serious or concentrate on her so hard. When she had finished, he sat back on his rear legs and thought for a second. Then he nodded and said, "yes, I will help."

"Of course, I will be coming too," said Imogen, "because you won't know anyone and two sets of eyes would be better." She surprised herself saying this, but then realised she really wanted go with him.

Roari was speechless, but before he could say anything a voice came from the corner of the bush beside them.

"And you will need someone to show you the most likely areas and tell you where to find the cohorts." Imogen quickly turned around and grinned at Corshus.

They both turned to Roari and looked expectantly. He frowned at them both and then nodded and smoke shot out from both sides of his mouth. "Yes and we can look all around the mountains and trees, because you two ...who are you?"

He stopped, suddenly realising he had never met an Undurbedder before.

"This is Corshus and somewhere is Norti."

"I'm here and I'm not being left behind."

There stood Norti, arms folded and looking very stern and determined.

"I've got to come to look after Corshus and Imogen." Corshus looked up to the sky, but before she could speak, Roari put his head to one side, thinking. He arched his long neck, stretched and spread out his huge wings, which formed a dark shadow over the children.

"Yes," he said, folding his wings again, "I should be able to carry you all without a problem. Easier than adult Undurbedders. That would be too much weight in one place."

He looked down at Imogen, "This is going to be a real adventure. But we will have to be careful." Imogen looked thoughtful, "You are right Roari, this is different from our other journeys isn't it," and stroking the base of his long neck, smiled a serious smile up at him. She then looked at the others and said, "We had better go and tell Wilmena what we want to do."

Then with Roari following, all three ran around to the front of the bush where the others had gathered. As Roari came into view, there was a communal gasp and some cries of fear from the villagers who, along with Wilmena, had gathered outside the front of the Speaking Hall. Everyone, including Roari, stood still.

The silence was finally broken by Wilmena, who smiled up at Roari. "You are welcome Dragon of Whenua O Nga Maama (country of white-topped mountains). We thank you for coming to our land. I have heard of your kin, but never seen one of your family before."

Roari shuffled about nervously, for he was not used to being addressed so formally. He concentrated and then bowed his head and mumbled "Kia Haruru Koe To Iwi ("May you and your people be blessed").

Wilmena smiled and asked if Imogen had explained the Land's need. Roari looked at Imogen and then replied that he had and was ready to fly and search for Bagsheela. But he then looked at the others and explained that he would be flying quite high so it was safe, but several pairs of eyes would help. He wanted to carry Imogen, Corshus and Norti. He explained that he could not carry any Watchers as they would be too heavy.

Wilmena's eyes narrowed and the children feared it would be a straight 'no'. But she remained silent and then nodded gently.

"Do you promise Roar i Dragononda nui ki te nui paowa, me te mura, to keep the children safe?" Roari was shocked that she knew his full Dragon name. He just nodded in agreement.

She turned to Leadser and the others. "I do not know of any creature that could attack the dragon. I do not sense danger for them if they are flying high above the ground". She looked to Leadser and the others, who nodded. And so it was decided.

Imogen and the others were so excited they hardly listened to the many instructions from parents and Watchers on what they must and mustn't do. But they gladly took the packs of food and drink they were offered for their journey. When all was ready, Leadser sat them down and explained where they needed to go and what to do in the event of seeing Bagsheela or any of her Followers.

"We do not know how long we have. But I think for your safety you must return by sunset two days hence. Do you understand? I fear that any later and Wilmena's power to protect the Land against Bagsheela will be weakened."

Turning to Roari she added, "She may be strong enough to be a threat, even to you." Leadser looked back with worry and concern towards Wilmena, who was lying back on her bed exhausted. She then looked at each one in turn.

"Be careful of yourselves and each other. This is no game and I fear what Bagsheela would do if she captured you and decided you threatened her plans."

The children and Roari suddenly forgot to be excited and a cold dread began to spread through them. They just looked at each other and nodded their agreement to Leadser. And then it was time to leave.

Roari lay down and Imogen who had flown on his back many times scrambled up, but even she found it difficult these days because he had grown so big. She had to help the others up. Corshus sat at the front, then Imogen as she was taller and could show them both how to fly on a dragon. Norti sat last, as he was the tallest and could see over the heads of the others.

"This is very different to riding a fox. Hold tight with your hands and legs, especially at the beginning when Roari gains height. Try to sway with the beat of his wings. Are we too heavy Roari?" Roari looked round at her and snorted smoke. "You forget I am nearly fully grown now Imogen! Too heavy!" he snorted again.

He looked down at the assembled villagers.

"You need to stand well away from me now," and slowly they shuffled back to leave the square in front of him clear. Then he spread his wings and gathered himself for the long flight.

Chapter 9 - The search begins

For a second, everything and everyone was quiet. Then Corshus and Norti gasped as they felt Roari leap into the air, his powerful muscles stretching and straining, his wings flapping and flapping, their tummies lurching as with each swishing beat of his wings they rose higher and higher into the sky.

Then they were soaring high above the village and countryside and their nervousness fell away. The air was full of cries of joy and shouting out about what was on the left and right and in front of them. Roari was laughing at and with them before shouting back to them, "Which way...which way?"

He had to circle the village before Corshus took the lead and called out instructions to Roari. Then all of them talked about what they should do.

Roari then started to flap more quickly to gain speed, before settling into his normal pace. Imogen was used to the sensation of speed. The rush of winds, the movement up and down between wing beats. No one spoke for a time and Imogen could sense the tension in both Corshus and Norti, for they were travelling far more quickly than the fleetest of foxes.

But then both of them began to relax and revel in the speed and height and power of the dragon beneath them. They were both shouting and pointing out landmarks to Imogen and Roari and each other. Their excitement was infectious, and Imogen laughed as she remembered her own joy that night when she had flown with Roari for the first time.

Dragons are so strong that they can fly without tiring and it was two hours later before they began to think of stopping. The countryside had begun to change and rolling fields became increasingly hilly, with rocks sticking out like teeth. Imogen looked up at the sun high above them in the sky and said, "Shall we stop now Roari, for some food?"

The others eagerly agreed, so he circled round and dropped down to a valley and river bank. Although they were tired and a bit sore, they quickly recovered as they ate their lunch. They knew time was precious.

But it didn't stop Imogen looking at her sandwich for a second. She had never seen a sandwich with layers of different coloured leaves and petals before. It looked a bit strange, but one bite and she was convinced it was the best lunch ever.

Corshus stood up as soon as she had finished and pointed out a snow covered peak in the distance to their left.

"Leadser said we should start near that peak. It's called End Point. She said we should fly west, following the valley along its base. They think Bagsheela must be along there somewhere. So, the cohorts will be spreading along its length."
"What is a cohort?" asked Imogen, having time now to think of what they really meant by it.

"It's a group of 15 to 20 Watchers. But Leadser is the head of all the Cohorts."

Corshus continued and sweeping her arm across the horizon said, "The forest and mountains stretch all the way to the flat lands over there in the far West." Norti and Imogen stood up beside her. "But that's a huge area. How can the Cohorts get to her and then back in time?" he wondered.

Corshus spoke solemnly. "I think it shows how worried and desperate they are."

They were silent for a moment. Then Roari spoke up.

"Well if they get the stone from her, we can fly it back to Wilmena, can't we. It means I will have to go as fast as I can and you will have to hold on very tight."

Corshus and Norti's ears dropped. "You mean that we haven't been going fast?" gulped Norti.

Roari laughed. "No, of course not. I wanted you to get used to being on my back and not falling off!"

They were very thoughtful and quiet as they climbed up again onto his back. All too soon they were quickly climbing and near enough to the woods to start looking in earnest.

Imogen said, "Roari, if you look ahead with Corshus, I can look to the left and Norti to the right." They all agreed to the plan.

They all felt Roari begin to increase his pace, but both Corshus and Norti were clearly relaxed about the quicker speed. All conversation died as they concentrated on looking down. End Point started to rise up in front of them.

Corshus suddenly shouted and excitedly pointed. "Look, a camp!"

They all strained to see and sure enough in a clearing were several foxes tied up next to five small, dome-shaped tents.

"Is it them!" cried out Imogen as they started to circle the area.

Just then there was a shout from the camp and two men appeared from the tents. They stood still and signalled for others to come out. They pointed and drew their swords, huddled together at the strange creature now circling above them.

"It must be one of the Cohorts, let's remember the landmarks here, so we can check it against the map later," said Norti. They all waved and Roari sank close enough for them to see and recognise Corshus and Norti.

The Watchers gradually, half-heartedly waved back, bemused by the sight of two of their children on this giant, flying animal above their heads. Roari blew out a huge plume of smoke in welcome. Corshus shouted back, "We will have to remember that they won't know about Roari so we will have to approach their camps slowly."

"I think we should we stop and explain what is happening," said Norti.

Imogen guessed he would enjoy the moment of importance. "I don't think we have the time," replied Corshus. "I think she is right Norti," added Imogen. "I think we need to carry on. Don't you, Roari?"

Roari looked around. "It is such a huge area to search, I think we must hurry on."

The others agreed. For whilst they were excited about finding a cohort and enjoyed their looks of puzzlement, in truth they were all a bit disappointed that it wasn't Bagsheela's camp. With one more circle past and shouts of goodbye, they flew on.

The Land beneath them was now becoming very hilly, covered in thick forest, but with clearings near the valley bottoms that revealed a wide and placid river, that wandered around the base of End Point.

And so the watching began in earnest. Roari glided along the valley and the hill side, occasionally beating his wings, but now mainly using the warm air to lift and carry him from hill top, to hill top. Sitting and concentrating on watching the ground hour after hour is tiring, when there is nothing to see except trees and hills. They privately all began to wonder if Bagsheela was there at all.

"A clearing!" shouted Corshus. Roari quickly turned and flapped his wings to gain height, so that they wouldn't be too visible from the ground to fly over it.

They all craned forward with excitement to see it and look out for any movement or sign of Bagsheela and her camp.

"I can't see anything, can you?" shouted Imogen. None of them could.

"What's that?" shouted Norti, pointing down to the far corner, "by the forest edge."

They all strained to look and Roari flew down nearer to get a better view.

As he circled round close to the treetops, Corshus said, "I think it's just a funny-shaped tree trunk. Yes, it is."

They all felt deflated.

Roari looked back at them. "Look at the grass. See how long it is. I don't think anything has crossed there for some time."

They all let out a sigh and Roari flapped his wings. Gently, they rose up and along the valley, looking for any signs of life. Sometimes a clearing would have animals in it and another time, they saw smoke, only to realise they had reached the next Cohort's camp.

By late afternoon, they were tired, sore and fed up. "My neck aches and my bum aches and my legs ache. They are obviously not here. Can't we stop for a bit?" sighed Norti.

Corshus snorted, "I knew you would lose interest. We have to carry on."

Norti leaned around Imogen. "That's alright for you, you've got the most comfortable seat."

Corshus turned round glaring, her ears flat along the back of the her head. But before she could speak, Imogen shouted.

"Look! Look up ahead. What's happening? Can you see, the trees! Look ahead at the tree tops! They are going brown!"

Corshus turned around and stared where Imogen was pointing. She gasped as though she had been hit.

"Norti, look what's happening to the trees!"

Roari started to climb and as he did so revealed the whole area in front of them. The forest wasn't a mixture of lush dark and light greens. It had different shades of green, but also mottled shades of browns mixed with patches of black.

"It must be Bagsheela's doing. That must be what Wilmena the Wise meant when she said she could feel it was damaging the Land," said Norti. "Do you think that means the Stone is down there somewhere?"

No one answered. They watched with dread as Roari flew towards the brown and green forest ahead. They were silent. The only sound was the beating of his wings, as he flew more urgently towards the damaged trees.

Corshus started to weep as she cried out, almost in pain, "Look, look, you can see it spreading. Look, tree after tree is beginning to turn!"

Roari banked, so that he was flying above where the line of trees separating the green healthy ones and those turning brown. Imogen leaned forward and hugged Corshus but she was right; Imogen could see the individual trees. Tree after tree was wilting. Their leaves were turning as though the whole of autumn was happening in one day.

Roari spotted a clearing ahead and when he was sure it was deserted, he landed so they could talk properly. As they stood around quietly not speaking, Imogen and Norti hugged each other for comfort and then they all lent against Roari's warm sides.

Corshus whispered, "At this rate, the whole the forest and beyond will soon be destroyed. We must find her. How can Bagsheela want this?"

She turned to face the others. Her tears of sadness dried up as she looked defiantly at them all.

"We have to find the stone and soon, before there is nothing left to save."

Imogen looked up and realised how low the sun was getting.

"Roari, at home, you can see in dark and so can I if I am with you. Will you be able to see in the dark here?"

Roari snuffled. "Oh Yes! I can see in the dark in any land. So, I think we should carry on. I'm not sure we can afford to wait until daylight. In fact," he continued snuffling with excitement, as an idea came to him, "Bagsheela won't know about being seen from above, so if we carry on and they have a fire, even a small one, we will be able to see it miles away."

Corshus and Norti listened, not quite sure what Roari meant about seeing in the dark.

But they both agreed that this deep in the forest, Bagsheela and her Followers could easily think it safe to have a small fire at night. So, it probably was a really good idea to fly on, even if they were tired and sore.

"Don't worry," said Imogen, "you will soon understand about being able to see after the sun sets". Puzzled but recognising now was not the time for explanations, they focused on having a mouthful of food and drink before setting off again.

It was starting to get cooler, so Roari was unable to rely on air thermals to glide. He beat his wings and settled into a steady rhythm. They watched the sun setting against the forest and mountainside. The light started to fade, but still there was no sign of Bagsheela. They were finding it harder and harder to see, when suddenly the light changed and became eerily clear. It wasn't exactly daylight, but they could see everything clearly. Corshus and Norti rubbed their eyes, unsure what was happening.

Imogen laughed. "It is strange isn't it. It's Roari's doing. I don't understand how you do it Roari. But it means we can see in the dark."

Norti interrupted her. "Look on your right, is that another clearing?"

"Where?" said the others, straining to see. "I can see it too!" cried Imogen. She pointed out a gap in the forest on the right in the distance.

But Corshus wasn't looking at the forest, she was looking at Imogen's arm.

"The necklace, look at the necklace Imogen, it's beginning to glow red!"

Imogen looked at her wrist and gasped. Corshus was right. The necklace she wore as a bracelet to make her small was pulsing a weak red colour. Stranger still, it was only the dark part that was pulsing red.

"Let me see" said Norti.

Imogen held it up for him to see.

"I think it's something to do with the stone. And look, as we fly towards that clearing, it's getting stronger. It's lighting us up. Cover it up Imogen or Bagsheela will see us!"

Imogen quickly covered it. But as they flew over the clearing, they realised nothing was moving, there wasn't anyone there. Roari carried on.

Soon Imogen could not resist peeking at the stone. The colour. It was definitely getting stronger.

She shouted to the others, "I think Norti is right, I think the stone will get brighter as we get closer to her and the stolen stone. Keep going forward Roari." Roari speeded up and Imogen kept checking the stone's colour. Corshus pointed to the middle distance. There wasn't a clearing, but there appeared to be a flickering light, a small night fire.

"It's them, I'm sure of it."

They all craned forward as Roari climbed higher so he could circle above them without being seen.

It was a small clearing. There was a primitive fence, holding a dozen or so foxes. Three small, domed tents and one large one dominated the open area. And there warming herself against the night air by the flickering fire was a woman. Even from their height, Imogen could see that she looked, like a much younger version of Wilmena. "It is her isn't it?" whispered Imogen.

The others nodded their agreement. They had found Bagsheela.

Chapter 10 - A plan is made

They circled the clearing. They could see that Bagsheela was giving instructions to her Followers, who were sitting in a group around the fire. They couldn't hear what she was saying but she was standing proudly in front of them, wearing a long cloak like Wilmena's, but instead of petals of many colours, hers seemed to be a mixture of browns and black. She stood tall and proud, but she looked unhappy and was angrily pointing at one of them.

Roari had been gliding around the campfire, but he now had to flap his wings to regain some height. But in the silence of the night, the sound must have carried. Two of the Watchers stood up and peered into the moonless sky, searching for the sound.

Roari turned and drifted gently away to a safer distance. Bagsheela and her Followers were listening and watching, but Bagsheela then turned back and started to talk again. The two who had stood up reluctantly sat down. Corshus spotted a tiny clearing nearby, she tapped Roari on the neck and pointed down. Roari nodded and drifted down silently towards it. Corshus and Norti gasped as they neared the ground, because they realised it wasn't grass they could see, but leaves, dead leaves.

Roari landed as gently as he could, but the crackling sound of his feet rustling through the piles of dead leaves was very noisy. They stayed perfectly still for a minute. They heard nothing, so slipped off his back. They stood looking around them. They had been so focused on the search for clearings, they had become almost used to the darkening of the leaves. But now, standing there, they could see how much damage Bagsheela was causing.

"The leaves Norti! All the leaves. They're falling off. They are not just changing colour. They are falling off; the trees must be dying."

"Don't the leaves ever come off here then Corshus?" Imogen asked. "Because at home they fall off many trees every year and then grow back the next year."

Corshus wiped her tears away and looked at Imogen with a confused expression. "No, they never fall. How can they? It... it must mean the trees are dying.

Norti, what is she doing, she is of the Land. Why would she want this?" She held out her arms to the dying forest around her. They looked around. The trees had lost nearly all their leaves. They could see through the trees and in the distance the glow of Bagsheela's fire.

Norti took a deep breath. "This is bad. I mean really bad. We don't have time to go back and find a Cohort to get the stone. I think we have to steal it." Corshus snorted. "Don't be stupid, how?" "Look around Corshus, look at the trees. They are dying," he hissed, "I don't think we have time to find or fetch a Cohort."

Corshus then took a deep breath. She nodded.

"You are right Norti. Think about her camp. She must have been planning this for ages. Its miles and miles away from any path. I think this camp has been set up before. It must have taken them all this time just to get here."

Norti replied, "Think how long it would take for a cohort to get here once we found the nearest one? We have to try and get it."

Imogen didn't know what to say. She wasn't a coward, but she was frightened by the thought of trying to take the stone. She had never taken or stolen anything in her life.

"I don't know how to get the stone," she said softly, "there are lots of them besides Bagsheela. And the stone, we don't know where it is." Corshus smiled at Imogen and then said, "I don't know how we can do it either, I just know Norti is right, we have to try. We don't have time."

They all went quiet, looked around at the falling leaves and listened to the distant creaking and rustling of the damaged trees.

Just then, there was a groan, a crack and a sound like a waterfall. Turning around, they could see a massive tree through the forest, leaning and leaning and then crashing to the ground. In the distance, there was another one. They held hands and backed up against Roari's sides.

"It's getting worse, the trees are falling!"

Then Roari took a sharp intake of breath. He had an idea and swished his tail in the leaves with excitement, which made then all gasp and hiss "SSSHHHH" at him. He dropped his head, and shamefully said sorry, but then grinned.

"I think I know how to rescue the stone," he snuffled more blue smoke as the others listened intently, "Wilmena said the stone is too heavy for one person to carry. It wasn't near the fire, it must be in the tent. I bet it's in the big tent. So, if I distract Bagsheela and her Followers, then you could sneak into the back of the tent and take it. Then we can fly it back to Wilmena."

"But if it's so heavy, how can we carry it out of the tent?" asked Imogen.

Norti looked around. "There should be branches and vines around for us to make a cradle." Corshus nodded in agreement, for all Undurbedd children were taught wood craft.

"But," said Corshus, "that won't get us into the tent, you need a knife to cut the leaf canvas." Roari opened his mouth and then shut it. "Oh! I hadn't thought of that," and seemed to deflate as his grand idea started to fall apart.

"But I have," said Norti proudly, getting a knife and scabbard out of his backpack.

"Norti!" exclaimed Corshus, "how could you be so stupid. You know only those training to be Watchers are allowed knives. You know knives lead to trouble."

Norti looked crestfallen and sheepish.

"But we need one, don't we?" he muttered.

"Well it's too late now. Just promise me you won't be so stupid again?" She crossed her arms, determined to be answered.

"Okay I promise, but it will be useful won't it?" "Yes and you know that is not the point." Corshus glared at a Norti, who sighed and nodded his head in agreement.

Roari excitedly said, "Remember, you won't be able to see in the dark once I have left you. I'll circle above you until you have gone around the camp to the back of the tent. Don't forget the foxes, I suppose they are easily disturbed."

He looked at Corshus and Norti, who both nodded. "So," he continued, "you will have to walk very carefully through the branches and leaves." At that point, another tree groaned and crashed to the ground.

Norti and Corshus quickly made a cradle of branches and vines to carry the stone back to their clearing and having agreed the plan again, Roari rose up above the trees and watched as the children set off towards the distant fire.

Chapter 11 - The Stone of Undurbedd

They hugged each other and then set off, aiming for the light of Bagsheela's fire. Imogen felt excited but nervous. It was a good plan, but she felt that lots could still go wrong. For a moment they could see perfectly, but as soon as Roari flew away, their night vision disappeared and they were left to see by the distant glow of Bagsheela's fire.

The forest was full of strange sounds, the crackle of leaves beneath their feet, the creaking and straining of dying trees. Imogen could see the pain in Corshus and Norti's eyes even in the moonlight. She looked up and smiled because although she couldn't see Roari anymore she could hear the reassuring beat of his wings.

They ran on. Time was critical and this far away, they were not afraid of alerting her Followers or the resting foxes.

Gradually the light grew and with it, the sound of the foxes quietly calling to each other mixed with the deeper voices of Bagsheela's Followers. Corshus, who was leading, signalled for them to stop. They could see Bagsheela standing in the middle. The Followers were also standing and looking up at the night sky. They were all dressed in browns and black, swords and knives hanging from their waists.

Imogen hoped all the Followers were around the campfire. She tried to count, but they were moving around too much to be sure.

She whispered, "It must be Roari they can hear. I think he must be trying to distract them." They could hear snatched words and voices.

"I heard it too. I think it was over there...NO! It's over here!"

"It sounds as though it's above us, but that makes no sense unless it's a giant bird!"

"It's the noise of the forest, it's confusing everything."

"What's happening Bagsheela, is this your doing?" Then they heard her voice. It felt harsh and cruel.

"This is not of my making. This is power of a different kind. I can feel it. Be on your guard."

Imogen asked, "Do you think they are all outside?"

Norti replied, "Just wait until Roari starts properly, I bet they will all be there then!"

He was so excited he started to talk normally. Corshus clipped his shoulder.

"Shush!"

"Sorry."

Corshus tapped them both on the shoulders and pointed. To their left was the domed tent. They looked at each other nervously. Then, hearts pounding, they grimly smiled at each other and set off.

They edged their way towards the tent, keeping well back into the forest. Although the forest was carrying sounds of trees groaning and falling, there were so many branches and twigs underfoot, that each step they made seemed to carry a noisy mix of rustling and snapping.

All three were constantly watching the Followers. Suddenly one turned around, as if she heard something. She stood still, staring in their direction, looking for the source of the noise. All three froze in horror. Had they been discovered? At that second there was huge ROOOAAARRRR! from across the clearing.

The Followers turned and ducked, drawing their swords. The foxes were tied to a circular fence. They were snarling and baying, restlessly pacing the enclosure, pawing the ground, eager to be away from this new and frightening menace.

The three ran quickly towards the big tent. All their worries of being quiet were forgotten. They knew the noise from the forest, Roari, the foxes and the shouts from the camp, meant they could not possibly be heard. They sighed in relief as they stepped round to the back and out of sight of Bagsheela and her Followers.

Roari continued to circle the trees, watching the children make their way towards the tent. He had seen one of the Followers stop and look in their direction, and quickly realised he had to cause a distraction. He continued to swoop and roar. Always without flame and high enough not to be seen in the low firelight, he knew this would cause maximum confusion.

As soon as he saw they were behind the tent he gathered his breath, swept down towards the dead trees on the opposite side of the clearing and blew flames at the tree tops, instantly igniting them.

Roari knew he would be visible then, but climbed high so they quickly lost sight of him. He swung round and flew down over the tent and roared at the tethered foxes. They were already frightened, but their training had kept them together.

But the sight of a huge dragon flying directly down and towards them was too much though. Snarling and howling, they scrambled to get over the fences, which suddenly and noisily collapsed under their combined weight. With the fence down, they rushed wildly across the clearing and into the trees beyond.

The Followers were running backwards and forwards, trying to catch them. Two Followers though stayed beside Bagsheela, back to back to protect her against the flying demon. Roari didn't want to hurt anyone or thing so he kept flying up and around the edge of the clearing furthest from the tent.

His plan was working perfectly. No one was near the tent. Norti had been watching from the edge and seeing the moment was perfect, took his knife and ripped a hole in the back of the tent from his head to the floor. They crept in. The open tent flap at the front meant the inside was lit up by the forest fire. There were blankets on the floor where some of the Followers slept, apart from one corner where a sheet hung down to separate them. But the stone wasn't to be seen.

"It must be behind that sheet. I bet that's Bagsheela's sleeping area," said Corshus. Bending double to avoid being seen, she ran over to it and pulled the sheet to one side. She stopped and looked in wonder. On the floor, beside the luxurious blankets and pillows was a large, oval shaped object. It was covered by a large square of shiny material. Woven into the cover were swirls and lines and runes of the purest gold thread. It shone and shimmered. Corshus felt the other two come up beside her and all three stared at it.

"This must be it," hissed Norti.

They all held their breath as Corshus slowly walked over and carefully lifted the cloth away.

There it sat. Pulsing a dark red, the colour of blood. The Stone of the Land. Wilmena's life stone.

Imogen thought it was the size of a rugby ball. It was as smooth as her own stone, but this one was covered in runes and swirls of even more detail than the cloth cover. One part remained dark and untouched by the red light of the rest of it. They all stood over it staring, even Corshus and Norti. For only when a child reached adulthood were they allowed to see and touch the stone and then only once as part of the coming of age ceremony.

"We must hurry," said Corshus. "Imogen, can you watch whilst Norti and I lift it onto the cradle?" Norti snorted, "I'll do that," and then gasped as he could barely lift it.

"Come on Norti, use your brain. Roll it onto the cradle and then we can lift it between us."

They stretched out the cradle and together managed to roll it onto the vines in the middle. They put the straps attached to each end of the two poles over their shoulders and lifted. The vines between the poles strained but took the weight of the stone. They staggered as they stood up and tried to adjust to the weight.

Gradually, they moved towards the opening at the back of the tent, carefully avoiding tangling their feet in the blankets.

"How can it weigh so much?" groaned Norti. "Just focus Norti, we have to hurry," Corshus answered through gritted teeth. In truth, it was almost too heavy for her too.

At the very moment, Corshus and Norti crossed the opening a tree top in flames exploded, lighting up the whole clearing and the interior of the tent. Bagsheela was looking all around the camp and sky, watching for intruders. Her eyes lit upon the tent and seeing Corshus' back, struggling with a weight, guessed what was happening.

"The stone!" she screamed, "they are stealing my stone," and leapt towards the open tent. She ran, sword in front of her, teeth bared. The children gasped and saw her rushing at them. They had seconds, only seconds to get out.

Imogen scrambled out of the back and held the torn flap open. Norti tried to quickly follow her but stumbled through the opening. The front of the pole caught on the ripped tent.

"Hurry!" screamed Corshus, looking over her shoulder.

Bagsheela neared the tent entrance with a Follower close behind her. She screamed with fury. Corshus turned back and mouthed a silent scream in reply as she looked into Bagsheela's hate-filled eyes. Then too quickly to follow, just as Bagsheela and the Follower reached the entrance, Corshus saw a huge shape cut out the light. Two massive claws appear behind the Bagsheela and the Follower, the claws grabbing them, their screams of surprise and fear, then the entrance collapse as a body fell onto it. Then, blackness.

Roari had dropped the Follower onto the tent front to stop others getting in. He banked sharply and beat his wings furiously to avoid the trees in front of him, straining with the effort of holding onto the squirming and screaming form of Bagsheela.

He suddenly felt a blow to his side. Bagsheela had hit him with her sword. But such was her fear and fury she had hit his scaly side, so it didn't cut him. She twisted, and reached back to thrust her sword into his soft belly.

Chapter 12 - The race for home

Roari waited until the last minute and dropped her, before she could strike again. She fell onto the top of a huge tree. It bent and swayed, its dying branches retaining little of their former strength. It began to topple and then as Bagsheela, eyes wide with fear and screaming her hate, watched as the tree top she clung onto crashed into its neighbour.

Branches scraped and scratched her, as she clung desperately onto her tree. It shivered and started to right itself. She looked around. The branches below had broken off. She was stuck there, 20 metres above the ground!

She looked down and howled as she spotted the children struggling out of the back of the tent with the stone on the cradle. Her Followers, spread across the clearing, had watched, motionless with disbelief as Roari had suddenly swooped down and picked up Bagsheela, only to drop her into the top of the highest tree.

Then they came to their senses when she pointed to the back of the tent and screamed, "Quickly you fools! My stone, at the back of the tent! They have my stone! Hurry, get them! Kill them! Get my Stone!"

Except for the stunned Follower on the tent roof, the remaining Followers reacted to her screeched command and began running towards the entrance. But Roari landed in front of the tent, spread out his wings and roared flames towards them. They staggered back with the heat from the flames, but unhurt. Roari started to walk towards them, then stopped, rose up on his hind legs and roared flame and fire at them. He roared so loudly that it echoed around the clearing and left them fearful of their lives.

The men and women Followers, brave in their own way, backed away. Roari started to move towards them. One and then two and then all of them began to run away from the fearsome beast. They didn't care about the desperate cries from above of, "Come back you cowards. What about me, have you forgotten your Leader?"

Roari turned back and saw the children slowly coming around the tent. They were grinning with excitement.

"That was wonderful Roari!" said Corshus.

"It was better than wonderful it was BRILLIANT!" said Norti, his eyes full of wonder and admiration.

Imogen glowed with pride. She ran up to him hugged him. Thank you," she said simply.

Roari swished his tail with pleasure and snuffled a cloud of smoke. "I was worried when she started to run to the tent, I didn't think I would get there in time!"

Then they laughed with sheer relief.

"Enjoy your moment of victory children, but I shall have my revenge on each and every one of you."

"Not from up there you won't!" shouted Norti. He laughed, but it was a hollow laugh and they all went quiet for a second.

"Yes, remember who you taunt, little man."
"We had better get going, I can see the Followers gathering in the tree line over there," said Corshus urgently.

Seeing the fresh danger, they quickly climbed onto Roari's back. The Followers realised what Roari was about to do. They spread out around him, raised their swords and charged at him. Roari sprayed fire from left to right to hold them back, but they knew this was their last chance. Braving the flames, they continued to rush him, shouting defiantly with swords out in front of them.

He roared fire again, but not as much this time. He did not wish to hurt them, just stop them. He picked up the stone with his front claws and leaped up into the air, furiously beating his wings. He then flew just above the sword of the lead Follower.

She threw her sword at Roari in a final act of desperation. Imogen saw the blade flashing in the flame light at it whirled towards her. She shut her eyes and tensed herself in horror, only to hear it bounce off Roari's sides and fall to the ground. She felt sickness and relief combined as she opened her eyes to look down, and then behind her.

They stood in a semi-circle where they had just been. With Roari's sight restored to her, Imogen looked across at Bagsheela as Roari began to circle the clearing. She was well and truly stuck in the top of the tree. She didn't look nearly so proud as she swayed around, hanging on grimly, her plans in ruins.

Roari headed away. Corshus looked back as well, but she was more concerned about the trees.

"The fire, it doesn't seem to be spreading. Maybe it was only those trees that are damaged the most, that will catch fire. Perhaps it is for the best, now Bagsheela has destroyed their lives and they are dying. How can she have wanted them destroyed?"

Roari interrupted her. "You must all hold on as tightly as possible now," he said, "I must fly as quickly as I can."

With that, they felt his muscles tighten and the beat of his wings increase. The wind in their hair grew fiercer. The children's thoughts and efforts were focused on hanging on and not slipping off. They were so tired that despite the soreness from sitting on a dragon's back and the effort of holding on, the knowledge that they were going home and the rhythmic beating of Roari's wings, meant keeping awake was the biggest worry. They tried talking, but the noise of the wind made it impossible.

After what seemed hours, Roari started to glide down and they realised that the land was flatter. "I need to rest," said Roari, "the weight of the three of you and the stone has made me very tired." The children quickly became livelier when they realised he was dropping down towards a Cohort's camp, the one they had seen and waved to earlier in the day.

The Cohort were initially very wary of the large dragon, despite the presence of Corshus and Norti on its back. But their caution quickly turned to surprise, then jubilation, as they realised Roari was holding the stone and was taking it back to Wilmena.

There followed a thousand questions, as the Cohort members wanted to know what had happened. Imogen was happy for Norti and Corshus to explain everything; she just grateful to sit down and accept a bowl of delicious hot stew and bread. She decided that it was even better than her Mum's. It made her a little home sick until she started to laugh as Norti's explanations, which became more and more extravagant, and Corshus' interruptions to explain what really happened, became more frequent.

Then they were wrapped up in blankets and before they realised it, were fast asleep. Roari needed to rest and had quickly curled his tail around his body, the stone firmly covered by his wings and legs. He fell fast asleep before they had finished their meal. He had not eaten, explaining Dragons ate less frequently than others.

As promised, the Cohort had watched over them and woken them to greet the chill of the dawn. All four were still very tired and sore, but Roari knew he would be able to complete the journey and all four knew they had to get back to Wilmena as soon as they could.

The Cohort were breaking camp and preparing their foxes to go and track Bagsheela, when Roari took off and headed across the green fields of the Land. Even here though, they could see the hurt that Bagsheela's attempts to bend the stone to her will had caused. The rose forests were beginning to droop, the river had begun to turn grey from blue and a host of other signs showed the sickness of the Land.

It was lunchtime and the sun was high in the sky when the familiar sight of the bushes that formed the village came into view. Never had they been so relieved as they were when Roari began to slow and glide down towards the centre of the village. He roared a welcome and Undurbedders streamed out to welcome them. But absent was Wilmena.

Leadser was at the front of the crowd of welcoming villagers. The joy on everyone's faces grew as they realised that not only had the children returned safely, but with the stone. Two Watchers rushed up with a wooden cradle, woven with patterns of gold along its side, to take the stone to the Speaking Hall where Wilmena had previously met them. As they walked behind Leadser through the crowd, Imogen felt her back patted again and again. Cheers were ringing in her ear. She could not believe it was only yesterday that they had started out.

All was quiet and hushed in the hall. Wilmena lay on her couch, propped up with pillows, but was clearly very ill. But her eyes sparkled and a small smile played on her face, as she saw what was on the cradle that was placed beside her. The villagers quietly filed in behind them and sat down on the floor in semi-circled rows, facing the bed and Wilmena.

Roari was too big to get in and so he was encouraged to go to the door. That way, he could put his neck and head inside and rest it on his from legs. The children were called forward to sit beside Leadser. Imogen asked if it would okay if she sat next to Roari. Leadser smiled. "Of course, you must, it is right and proper that you do so." So, Imogen stepped through the villagers and took her place next to Roari, resting against his neck.

The assembly was quiet. Imogen could sense the worry and tension in the atmosphere. The fear that the stone had been returned too late, but the hope that perhaps, there was still time. Wilmena stretched out her hand and rested it on the stone.

At first nothing happened. Then Wilmena began to gently smile and the crowd gasped as the stone started to turn blue and then pulse with all the colours of the rainbow. At first it was dull and hardly noticeable and then it became brighter and brighter, shining through Wilmena's hand and filling the hall with its colour. A low hum began and Imogen wondered where it had come from. She looked with increasing amazement as it became clear that it was from the stone itself.

The hum grew and grew in intensity, until Imogen and many others had to put their hands around their eyes. Then just as quickly it began to fade and as it did, Wilmena began to sit up and then rise. Except, this was not an old lady at the end of life. The years had fallen away from her and she stood, tall and proud, full of life and joy.

She smiled at Imogen across the hall and then leant forward to take Corshus and Norti's hands and help them up. She turned them around to face everyone, a hand on each of their shoulders.

"Imogen, Roari, Corshus and Norti," she stopped to smile, her warmth and kindness radiating out from her.

"Never has such a peril been faced by us before. But for your courage, I and the Land would have been lost. But now, I feel the Land is being healed by the stone as I have been. Fetch food and drink for them all and let us hear their story and ensure their tale is remembered not just by us, but by the generations that follow."

And so, between mouthfuls of food (which included several large baskets of fish for Roari) and with much embarrassment for the children and sighs and gasps and many, many questions from the villagers, their story was told.

The sun was nearing the horizon when they had told their tale for the final time. Wilmena stood and addressed them all.

"We must let them rest. Imogen, your time with us here draws to an end. For whilst are Lands are attached, it is still night time in your country and you must return soon."

And so Corshus Norti together with Imogen and Roari climbed the hill to the Doors of Shade, where they had begun their adventure. This time Leadser and some of the Watchers walked with them, as a salute to Imogen and Roari's bravery.

"It is time I went home as well," said Roari when they reached it. They all hugged him and one another. Then they stood back as with a flash, a cloud of smoke and a rush of warm air, Roari vanished.

The others walked wearily to the door. They all wished Imogen farewell and the three friends went through the door to the foot of her bed. There were few words left and so they just hugged each other again. Corshus quickly undid the bracelet from Imogen's wrist and this time she started to grow straight away. Before she realised it, she was her full size. Imogen knelt down and Norti and Corshus touched her hands, before the two of them ran back under the bed.

Imogen was so tired, but she still managed to smile as she lay down and wondered if she would see them again. She smiled again, because she was sure that day would come, and soon.

The End